STAR WARS REBELS™

HEAD-TO-HEAD

PABLO HIDALGO

SCHOLASTIC INC.

SCHOLASTIC
www.scholastic.com

Published by Scholastic Inc., 557 Broadway, New York, NY 10012; Scholastic Canada Ltd., Markham, Ontario

Scholastic and associated logos are trademarks of Scholastic Inc.

No part of this book may be reproduced, stored in a retrieval system, or transmitted in any form or by any means, electronic, mechanical, photocopying, recording, or otherwise, without the prior permission of Scholastic Inc.

Produced by becker&mayer!
11120 NE 33rd Place, Suite 101
Bellevue, WA 98004
www.beckermayer.com

becker&mayer!
BOOK PRODUCERS

If you have questions or comments about this product, please visit www.beckermayer/customerservice and click on Customer Service Request Form.

Edited by Delia Greve
Designed by Rosanna Brockley
Design assistance by Sam Dawson and Scott Richardson
Production management by Tom Miller

Special thanks to Joanne Chan Taylor, Troy Alders, Leland Chee, and Carol Roeder at Lucasfilm.

Printed, manufactured, and assembled in Jefferson City, MO, USA

First printing, September 2014

10 9 8 7 6 5 4 3 2   14 15 16 17 18 19/0

ISBN 978-0-545-74642-7

13673

Characters, creatures, and vehicles from *Star Wars Rebels* are pitted against one another in the greatest matchups ever imagined! For each duel, you'll find all the stats and details you'll need to decide who you think will win. The last page features the experts' ruling on every battle.

THE BATTLES

SPOTLIGHT ON
LOTHAL

It is a dark time in the galaxy. . . .

The Republic is only a memory; the Empire now rules the galaxy. When the Emperor rose to power, he declared a new age of peace and justice. For a time, the galaxy breathed a sigh of relief that the chaos and destruction of the Clone Wars had finally ended. But in the years that followed, it became clear the Emperor meant to impose order through oppression and cruelty. The Galactic Empire grew to be a powerful and seemingly unstoppable force.

To fuel its expansion, the Empire took control of some independent planets in the Outer Rim that were rich in resources. The remote world of Lothal, bountiful in grasslands and minerals, at first welcomed the attentions of the Empire, which promised a bright future. But the Imperial occupation soon created harsh conditions for Lothal's farmers, factory workers, and miners. When the locals protested, the demonstrations were swiftly stopped.

Now the people of Lothal live in fear. Stormtroopers march the streets and TIE fighters streak the sky. It is a time for freedom fighters to unite and inspire, to show the citizens of Lothal that the Empire can be pushed back, and perhaps, someday, even defeated.

It is a time of rebellion.

EZRA BRIDGER ⊙ VS. IMPERIAL STORMTROOPER

Ezra Bridger has never known a life without the Imperial occupation. He grew up in the streets of Capital City, fending for himself. Ezra's quick wits and reflexes have kept him ahead of the Empire, but his luck doesn't last forever. A stormtrooper catches Ezra stealing Imperial supplies, and a fight begins!

EZRA BRIDGER

A fourteen-year-old streetwise urchin, Ezra has lived on his own for most of his life. He has charm, strong survival instincts, and remarkable reflexes because he can see things an instant before they happen. Though Ezra doesn't know it, he is Force-sensitive.

INFO

Homeworld	Lothal
Affiliation	Rebel
Species	Human
Height/Weight	1.65 meters/50 kilograms
Weapons	Custom-modified stun-sting slingshot
Special move	Dodge-and-roll

STATS

Intelligence	Strength	Agility	Damage	Control	Courage
5.5	5	8	4	6	8

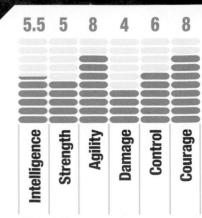

THE SHOWDOWN

In a crowded marketplace, Ezra tries to snatch the spare hand-comlink the stormtrooper keeps on his belt. The trooper spots the would-be thief in the reflection of a glass vendor's stand. The trooper chases Ezra, cornering him in an alleyway. The stormtrooper orders the boy to halt and put his hands up, giving Ezra the perfect opportunity to arm the stun-sting slingshot he carries on his wrist.

STORMTROOPER

After the Clone Wars, the Emperor put out a call for young patriots to volunteer for duty as Imperial stormtroopers. The Emperor created new soldiers absolutely loyal to him. The fighting forces wear eighteen-piece plastoid armor over a black body glove, and their faces are entirely concealed behind their distinctive helmets.

STATS

Intelligence	5
Strength	6
Agility	5
Damage	6
Control	5
Courage	8

INFO

Homeworld	Various, including Lothal
Affiliation	Galactic Empire
Species	Various
Height/Weight	Average 1.83 meters/80 kilograms
Weapons	E-11 blaster rifle
Special move	Targeted strike

Who wins? See page 64.

The Imperial Academy on Lothal shapes the next generation of stormtroopers. Young cadets undergo drills to make them obedient, and strip away their individuality. This makes Sabine Wren—who has a passion for creative expression—see red. When she breaks into the Academy to plant a paint bomb, she crosses paths with Commandant Aresko.

SABINE WREN

An energetic saboteur, Sabine is an expert at customizing and maintaining technology and weaponry. She specializes in creating explosives that leave a signature mark, the birdlike calling card of the Rebel group. Her clothes are often spattered with paint, though she keeps her helmet—a Mandalorian helmet she inherited—spotless.

INFO

Homeworld	Mandalore
Affiliation	Rebel
Species	Human
Height/Weight	1.7 meters/52 kilograms
Weapons	Twin blaster pistols; explosive charges
Special move	Martial arts

STATS

Intelligence	Strength	Agility	Damage	Control	Courage
7.5	6	7	5	7	9

THE SHOWDOWN

Sabine knows the standardized layout of the Academy, and sneaks her way into the upper levels. She plants her magnetized paint bomb on the wall of the head office, right next to a holographic portrait of Commandant Aresko. The commandant makes an unscheduled return to admire his hologram, and draws his blaster upon seeing the helmeted intruder.

COMMANDANT ARESKO

Imperial officer Cumberlyn Aresko believes the Empire to be the pinnacle of civilization: a system of government that properly rewards brilliance as great as his! Though he boasts frequently of his skills and genius, his lofty position as head of the Lothal Imperial Academy can really be credited more to favors from friends and allies within the Empire.

STATS

Intelligence	6.5
Strength	5
Agility	5
Damage	6
Control	5
Courage	6

INFO

Lothal	**Homeworld**
Galactic Empire	**Affiliation**
Human	**Species**
1.89 meters/80 kilograms	**Height/Weight**
Blaster pistol	**Weapons**
Academy uppercut	**Special move**

Who wins? See page 64.

A well-muscled Lasat, Zeb respects how imposing a brawny form and a booming voice can be. He also knows a bully when he meets one. When the sound of Imperial Taskmaster Grint's gruff voice bossing around a trembling spaceport technician reaches his ears, Zeb's temper starts to boil. He decides it's time to take the burly Imperial's confidence down a few pegs.

GARAZEB "ZEB" ORRELIOS

A grumpy Lasat with excellent fighting skills, Zeb is happiest when punching stormtroopers. The Empire conquered his people, but he escaped thanks to his brains and good luck. There are not many Lasat left in the galaxy, and Zeb fights for his people as well as all those who cannot.

INFO

Homeworld	Lasan
Affiliation	Rebel
Species	Lasat
Height/Weight	2.1 meters/115 kilograms
Weapons	Lasat bo-rifle
Special move	Whirlwind throw

STATS

Intelligence	Strength	Agility	Damage	Control	Courage
5.5	10	8.5	7	6.5	10

Zeb's strong arms and handlike feet let him stealthily climb over the awnings overhead, well beyond Grint's beady little eyes. When the beefy Imperial pauses for breath after shouting, Zeb pounces. The Lasat's first dropkick sends Grint reeling, but the Imperial officer is no lightweight. Grint tugs the bill of his cap down, cracks his knuckles, and charges.

TASKMASTER MYLES GRINT

The Empire's goal of ruling through strength and fear appeals to Taskmaster Grint's mean-spirited nature. He enjoys terrorizing those who can't fight back, such as young Imperial cadets, Lothal farmers, and inner-city shopkeepers.

STATS

Intelligence	5.5
Strength	7.5
Agility	4
Damage	6.5
Control	6
Courage	7

INFO

Lothal	**Homeworld**
Galactic Empire	**Affiliation**
Human	**Species**
1.94 meters/95 kilograms	**Height/Weight**
E-11 blaster rifle	**Weapons**
Tackle and grapple	**Special move**

Who wins? See page 64.

KANAN JARRUS **VS.** THE INQUISITOR

It is a dangerous time to be Force-sensitive. By executing Order 66, the Emperor's plotting resulted in the overnight extinction of the Jedi Knights. Kanan Jarrus is one of the few survivors. By using his Jedi abilities to help others, he draws the attention of one of the Emperor's most sinister agents.

KANAN JARRUS

Kanan serves as the field sergeant for his small band of rebels, formulating strategies and commanding missions against the Empire. Keeping his identity as a Jedi survivor a secret means having to wear his lightsaber in pieces on his belt, but he can quickly assemble the weapon when emergencies call for it.

INFO

Homeworld	Unknown
Affiliation	Rebel
Species	Human
Height/Weight	1.91 meters/80 kilograms
Weapons	Gunslinger blaster pistol, lightsaber
Special move	Behind-the-back parry and strike

STATS

Intelligence	Strength	Agility	Damage	Control	Courage
6.5	8	8	7	7.5	10

THE SHOWDOWN

The Inquisitor's ashen face twists into a wicked grin. Kanan's ordinarily cocky personality suddenly becomes deadly serious. Their lightsaber blades extend, and the Inquisitor coldly examines Kanan's stance to figure out what fighting style Kanan uses. Even during the battle, the Inquisitor picks apart Kanan's abilities as a fighter.

THE INQUISITOR

A chilling interrogator and tireless investigator, the Inquisitor has been tasked with seeking out any Jedi survivors. The grim-looking Pau'an carries a unique ring-hilted, double-bladed lightsaber weapon he can easily spin in combat. Though the Inquisitor can use the Force, his sharp, quick mind is the most threatening of his abilities.

STATS

Intelligence	9.5
Strength	8.5
Agility	8.5
Damage	8
Control	9
Courage	10

INFO

Homeworld	Unknown, presumably Utapau
Affiliation	Galactic Empire
Species	Pau'an
Height/Weight	1.98 meters/80 kilograms
Weapons	Modified double-bladed lightsaber
Special move	Spinning lightsaber throw

Who wins? See page 64.

13

If Hera Syndulla had to tangle with a TIE fighter pilot, she'd much prefer it to be in the skies over Lothal. But her starship, the *Ghost*, is on the other end of the spaceport, and she's got to stop this Imperial pilot from running to his nearby craft and calling for backup.

HERA SYNDULLA

The pilot of the *Ghost*, Hera's main role is "getaway driver" for the rebels during their various schemes and heists. She is sensible, reliable, and a true believer in the cause of freedom. In addition to being an ace pilot and a good shot, her Twi'lek gift of grace gives her excellent agility in combat.

INFO

Homeworld	Ryloth
Affiliation	Rebel
Species	Twi'lek
Height/Weight	1.76 meters/50 kilograms
Weapons	Hold-out blaster
Special move	Acrobatic wall-run and flip

STATS

Intelligence	Strength	Agility	Damage	Control	Courage
8	5.5	7	5	7.5	10

THE SHOWDOWN

The pilot runs at full speed to the spaceport launch pad where his **TIE** fighter is refueling, but **Hera** catches up with him and sends him tumbling with a sliding kick to his ankle. The pilot tucks and rolls. It's close range now. The TIE pilot has to decide if he should grab for his blaster pistol, or lunge toward **Hera** and fight her hand to hand.

TIE FIGHTER PILOT

Replacing the clone pilots of the Republic, the fighter pilots of the Imperial Starfleet are the product of rigorous academy training. In this era of Imperial dominance, TIE pilots rarely encounter comparable resistance, so they tend to be insufferably cocky.

STATS

Intelligence	6
Strength	6
Agility	5
Damage	5
Control	7
Courage	7

INFO

Homeworld	Various, including Lothal
Affiliation	Galactic Empire
Species	Various
Height/Weight	1.83 meters/80 kilograms
Weapons	E-11 blaster rifle
Special move	Academy martial arts

Who wins? See page 64.

CHOPPER (VS.) LOTHAL ASTROMECH DROID

During a visit to Old Jho's pitstop on Lothal, Chopper rolls over to the recharge terminal to top off his power packs. A clear-domed Lothal astromech is parked at the socket, waiting for his indicator to flip to fully charged. Impatient, Chopper chirps for the droid to move, and then things turn ugly.

CHOPPER

Chopper (or C1-10P) is an eccentric astromech droid tasked with keeping the rebels' ship running. He is an older model C1 unit that has been rebuilt and patched together from other droid parts over the years. This has made him very cranky. Chopper is a grumpy droid who doesn't seem to like anyone.

INFO

Homeworld	Unknown
Affiliation	Rebel
Manufacturer	Unknown
Droid Type	Astromech droid
Height/Weight	0.99 meters/32 kilograms
Weapons	Electroshock prod, arc welder
Special move	Shock

STATS

Intelligence	Strength	Agility	Damage	Control	Courage
4.5	5	4	4	5	7

Chopper squawks and waves the grasping arms that extend from his domed head. The Lothal droid simply locks his wheels in defiance. Chopper charges, forcefully knocking the astromech away from the recharge station. However, the now fully-charged native droid extends its crackling electroshock prod while calling out a challenge. Chopper does the same.

LOTHAL ASTROMECH DROID

Though Lothal is remote, it is not without modern technology. Local firms, founded by colonists ages ago, keep pace with technological developments. Though the astromech droids found in the system may not be on the same level as the latest droids from Industrial Automaton, they are capable machines.

STATS

4	5	4	4	4	4
Intelligence	Strength	Agility	Damage	Control	Courage

INFO

Lothal	**Homeworld**
Independent	**Affiliation**
Lothal Logistics Limited	**Manufacturer**
Astromech droid	**Droid Type**
1.04 meters/32 kilograms	**Height/Weight**
Electroshock prod, arc welder	**Weapons**
Shock	**Special move**

Who wins? See page 64.

IG-RM THUG DROID (VS.) OLD JHO

As if life under the Empire wasn't bad enough, the citizens of Lothal have to deal with criminals as well. Like the cowards they are, many of these gangs leave it to droids to do their dirty work. A towering IG-RM thug droid stomps its way up to Old Jho's bar, demanding payment to ensure nothing violent happens to the Ithorian's saloon.

IG-RM THUG DROID

The destruction caused by battle droids during the Clone Wars led the Empire to outlaw droids solely built for warfare. However, sneaky companies like Halowan Laboratories continue to produce combat models like the IG-RM, and reclassify them as security units.

INFO	
Homeworld	Various
Affiliation	Broken Horn gang
Manufacturer	Halowan Laboratories
Droid Type	IG-RM bodyguard and enforcer droid
Height/Weight	2.09 meters/140 kilograms
Weapons	Blaster rifle, electrostaff
Special move	Staff twirl

STATS	
Intelligence	4
Strength	9
Agility	5
Damage	7
Control	6
Courage	6

THE SHOWDOWN

From behind the counter, Old Jho—speaking through a device that translates the Ithorian language into recognizable words—tells the droid the leader of the Broken Horn owes *him* money anyhow. The droid is either malfunctioning or doesn't understand this response, and smashes his powerful arms into the counter's surface.

OLD JHO

Old Jho is a longtime settler on Lothal who watched Capital City grow from a sleepy trading post to a center for Imperial administration. He maintains a saloon and docking bay on the outskirts of the city. Jho keeps his ears open for any chatter he thinks would benefit his most loyal customers, including rebels looking to cause trouble for the Empire.

STATS

Intelligence	8
Strength	6
Agility	4
Damage	5
Control	5
Courage	6.5

INFO

Homeworld	Ithor
Affiliation	Independent
Species	Ithorian
Height/Weight	1.99 meters/90 kilograms
Weapons	Hunting blaster
Special move	Under-the-counter blaster draw

Who wins? See page 64.

EXPLORE THE GHOST

The rebel crew on Lothal gets around in the *Ghost*, a midsized freighter that functions both as their transport and home base of operations. The diamond-shaped ship is constantly moving in the space around Lothal, sometimes setting down in the wilderness, other times docking at friendly port facilities run by allies who don't ask too many questions.

THE SHIP

- Its forward bubble-like cockpit has a gun turret directly beneath it.

- The ship also sports a bubble gunport on its underside with a full 360-degree sweep.

- Access to the ship is easy for the crew with a retracting ramp under the cockpit.

- In addition to internal cargo space, the ship has a recessed area on its belly where it can carry cargo pods.

LIVING QUARTERS

The *Ghost*'s crew customized their cabins to make them as homey as possible. Hera and Kanan have their own separate quarters. Zeb and Ezra share a cabin uncomfortably, while Sabine has a room of her own, which she decorates. Chopper mostly stays in the engine room. Common areas include a dining mess and a crew rec area with a holographic chess table.

ITS NAME

The ship gets its name from the special countermeasure systems and engines that make the ship hard to spot on sensors. It's not a cloaked ship (no ship this small would have a cloaking device), but it is sneaky: Its randomizing transponder system can help disguise it from Imperial scanners.

THE PHANTOM

What makes the *Ghost* unique is that it also has a single-person fighter called the *Phantom*. The small fighter docks into the ship's tail section—making the *Ghost* two ships in one.

GHOST VS. TIE FIGHTER

Although the small rebel group led by Kanan and Hera concentrates its operations on Lothal, they do travel aboard the *Ghost* to nearby systems to make money smuggling supplies. In order to deliver this cargo to safe drop points, the *Ghost* must avoid Imperial patrols.

GHOST

On the surface, the *Ghost* resembles a stock VCX-100 freighter, with various light weapons that won't attract Imperial attention. Hera's expert piloting and Kanan's uncanny skill with the laser cannons make the *Ghost* a surprise for overconfident Imperial pursuers.

INFO

Manufacturer	Corellian Engineering Corporation
Affiliation	Rebel
Type	Modified VCX-100 light freighter
Size	43.9 meters long
Weapons	1 dorsal laser turret; 2 forward laser cannons; 2 rear laser cannons
Top speed	1,025 kph (in atmosphere)

STATS

Control	Hull	Maneuver	Speed	Firepower
5	4.5	6	6	5

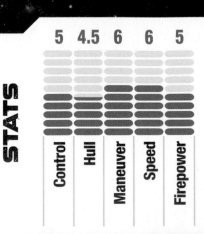

THE SHOWDOWN

As the *Ghost* lifts off from a secret drop point, it is spotted by a lone TIE fighter on a recon patrol. The TIE fighter makes for higher altitude to race back to Imperial headquarters. The *Ghost* must stop the TIE before more Imperials arrive. The TIE pilot is eager to fight, so once both ships are in space, the battle begins.

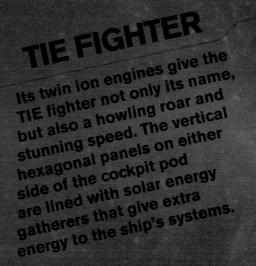

TIE FIGHTER

Its twin ion engines give the TIE fighter not only its name, but also a howling roar and stunning speed. The vertical hexagonal panels on either side of the cockpit pod are lined with solar energy gatherers that give extra energy to the ship's systems.

STATS

	Control	Hull	Maneuver	Speed	Firepower
	5	5	6.5	7	6

INFO

Sienar Fleet Systems	**Manufacturer**
Galactic Empire	**Affiliation**
Twin ion engine space superiority fighter	**Type**
5.33 meters long	**Size**
2 laser cannons	**Weapons**
1,200 kph (in atmosphere)	**Top speed**

Who wins? See page 64.

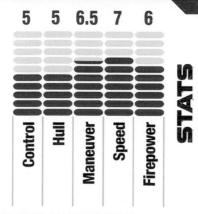

IMPERIAL SPEEDER BIKE (VS.) AT-DP

More than once, the rebels have stolen an Imperial speeder bike—the open-air vehicle makes for easy theft. The rebels usually ditch the bike quickly after taking it to prevent the Empire from tracking, but the heroes try to leave a lasting mark by using the bike's weapons against their enemy.

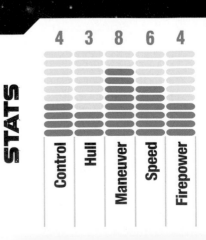

IMPERIAL SPEEDER BIKE

The speeder bike pilot reclines on a low-slung padded seat that sits above the engine. The bike's forward steering vanes are at the end of telescoping stalks. When extended, these vanes act as cooling surfaces for the built-in, double-laser cannons on the front of the craft.

INFO

Manufacturer	Aratech Repulsor Company
Affiliation	Galactic Empire
Type	614-AvA speeder bike
Size	3.98 meters long
Weapons	Twin forward facing laser cannons
Top speed	375 kph

STATS

Control	Hull	Maneuver	Speed	Firepower
4	3	8	6	4

THE SHOWDOWN

Sabine Wren needs to buy time for her fellow rebels to escape as an AT-DP closes in. After a shootout with stormtroopers, a speeder bike is left without a rider. Sabine leaps onto it, and fires up its thrusters. She circles the walker, drawing fire from its main cannon. She takes a few shots, but they strike harmlessly against the walker's thick skin.

AT-DP

Though not as imposing as some walkers, the towering AT-DP is well suited for maintaining order on city streets or in tall grass fields. The walker's armored head holds two crew members. The driver sits up front, while the gunner sits behind, operating a ball turret-mounted laser cannon that packs a devastating punch.

STATS

5	8	3	4	6
Control	Hull	Maneuver	Speed	Firepower

INFO

Kuat Drive Yards	**Manufacturer**
Galactic Empire	**Affiliation**
All Terrain Defense Pod	**Type**
11.64 meters tall	**Size**
1 laser cannon	**Weapons**
90 kph	**Top speed**

Who wins? See page 64.

JUMPSPEEDER (VS.) RGC LANDSPEEDER

As the biggest military force in the galaxy, the Empire limits the trade of weapons and supplies that can be used against them. Thus, rebels and criminals alike make the most of whatever equipment they can find, including civilian-issued vehicles like speeders designed for the sporting lifestyle.

JUMPSPEEDER

Originally developed as emergency craft for the Jedi Order and regional military patrols, the jumpspeeder design was repurposed for civilian use after the Clone Wars. The bike can fold down into a compact size for easy stowing, a feature that makes it very popular among young thrillseekers.

INFO

Manufacturer	Kuat Vehicles
Affiliation	Civilian
Type	Stowable *Undicur*-class jumpspeeder
Size	1.84 meters long (fully extended)
Weapons	None
Top speed	250 kph

STATS

Control	Hull	Maneuver	Speed	Firepower
6	2	7	5	1

THE SHOWDOWN

A thief has stolen a fuel cell intended for the *Ghost* and loaded it into his RGC landspeeder. Sabine spots the bandit streaking down the side streets of Capital City and jumps aboard a tiny jumpspeeder to chase him down. Neither vehicle is armed, so the thief must use his hand blaster. Likewise, all Sabine has are her blaster pistols.

RGC LANDSPEEDER

A classic design that has changed little over the years, the RGC speeder chassis is one that can be spotted darting across the skies of Coruscant. To make it affordable to inhabitants of outer worlds like Lothal, its cloud-climbing repulsors have been downgraded to a ground-hugging landspeeder model.

STATS

Control	Hull	Maneuver	Speed	Firepower
4	4	6	5.5	1

INFO

SoroSuub Corporation	**Manufacturer**
Civilian	**Affiliation**
RGC-18 landspeeder	**Type**
6.26 meters long	**Size**
None	**Weapons**
300 kph	**Top speed**

Who wins?
See page 64.

The Wookiees, fiercely loyal to the ideals of the Republic, are now viewed with suspicion by the Empire. An Imperial freighter serving as an orbital patrol vessel intercepts a Wookiee gunship, and a tense confrontation erupts into a space battle.

WOOKIEE GUNSHIP

Though the Wookiees are a technologically advanced culture, they prefer to explore their own forest world rather than the far corners of space. Thus, their spacefleet is limited, but what vessels they do have are compact and loaded with weapons.

INFO		
Manufacturer	Appazanna Engineering Works	
Affiliation	Wookiee	
Type	Modified attack gunship	
Size	43.9 meters long	
Weapons	Three double-laser cannon gunpods	
Top speed	950 kph (in atmosphere)	

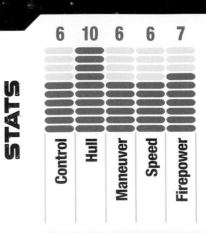

STATS

	6	10	6	6	7
	Control	Hull	Maneuver	Speed	Firepower

THE SHOWDOWN

The Wookiees are fortunate the freighter is not currently carrying TIE fighters on its belly. As the Imperial crew calls for its TIE fighters to return, the freighter is all that stands in the way of freedom. In characteristic Wookiee fashion, the gunship crew howls and bares their teeth, charging straight at the enemy.

IMPERIAL FREIGHTER

Built on a frame developed for civilian freighters, the Imperial freighters have more armor plating, and additional laser cannon turrets, and can dock smaller external craft. They often serve as a mobile platform for launching short-range TIE fighter patrols, or for carrying AT-DP walkers into position.

STATS

5	15	4	5	7
Control	Hull	Maneuver	Speed	Firepower

INFO

Corellian Engineering Corporation	**Manufacturer**
Galactic Empire	**Affiliation**
Modified Gozanti cruiser	**Type**
63.76 meters long	**Size**
1 dorsal double laser turret; 1 ventral single laser turret	**Weapons**
1,025 kph (in atmosphere)	**Top speed**

Who wins? See page 64.

Lothal's importance to the Empire means there is an Imperial Star Destroyer on permanent system patrol. Only the most daring scoundrels would attempt to outrun an Imperial blockade. A C-ROC carrier ship, filled with stolen ore, makes a foolhardy run for open space.

C-ROC CARRIER SHIP

The C-ROC carrier ship not only has the versatile Gozanti freighter frame as a foundation, but also has expanded its cargo capacity with open-bed platforms to carry secured containers. To propel these heavy loads are five robust engine pods that allow blockade-running captains speedy getaways.

INFO

Manufacturer	Corellian Engineering Corporation
Affiliation	Independent
Type	Modified Gozanti cruiser
Size	73.91 meters long
Weapons	1 dorsal laser turret; 2 forward laser cannons; 2 rear laser cannons
Top speed	1,200 kph (in atmosphere)

STATS

	Control	Hull	Maneuver	Speed	Firepower
	6	25	2	7	6

THE SHOWDOWN

The smuggler captain of the C-ROC ignores the calls from the Empire to halt, and diverts as much power to the engines as she can. She randomizes thrust between the five engine pods, giving the freighter a wildly unpredictable path that Imperial gunners can't track. She's less than a minute from the hyperspace jump point. Can she make it past the blockade?

IMPERIAL STAR DESTROYER

The Empire's imposing warship is covered with turbolaser and ion cannon batteries, which are designed to take out other large-scale capital ships. That's not all. Its holds are filled with TIE fighters and other combat craft.

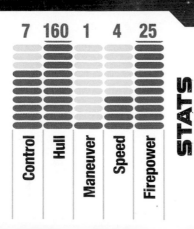

STATS

7	160	1	4	25
Control	Hull	Maneuver	Speed	Firepower

INFO

Kuat Drive Yards	**Manufacturer**
Galactic Empire	**Affiliation**
Imperial-class Star Destroyer	**Type**
1,600 meters long	**Size**
60 turbolaser cannons; 60 heavy ion cannon emplacements; 10 tractor beam projectors	**Weapons**
975 kph (in atmosphere)	**Top speed**

Who wins? See page 64.

To hide from Imperial attention, the Broken Horn criminal syndicate uses modified civilian vehicles. However, the Empire has stepped up its random patrols of Capital City traffic and has found one of Cikatro's fleet of speeders loaded with stolen blaster pistols.

V-35 LANDSPEEDER

Commonly found on Outer Rim planets like Lothal or Tatooine, the outdated and inexpensive V-35 landspeeder is characterized by its angular nose, raised repulsorlift thrusters, and large barrel-shaped power plant.

INFO

Manufacturer	SoroSuub Corporation
Affiliation	Broken Horn gang
Type	V-35 Courier landspeeder
Size	7.64 meters long
Weapons	None
Top speed	120 kph

STATS

Control	Hull	Maneuver	Speed	Firepower
5	4.5	6	6	5

THE SHOWDOWN

The already-nervous Broken Horn gunrunner panics; he does not want to confront a disappointed Cikatro Vizago. He throttles the V-35's triple bank of engines, and attempts to charge past the troop transport, which opens fire. With little to lose, the speeder driver flies directly at the transport, hoping the Imperial will pull out of the way.

IMPERIAL TROOP TRANSPORT

The brick-shaped Imperial Troop Transport is a humbling sight on Lothal. The planet's citizens know the floating tank might be filled with half a dozen stormtroopers, and that the six compartments on the outer hull may carry additional troopers, or worse—prisoners bound in open view as a warning to others.

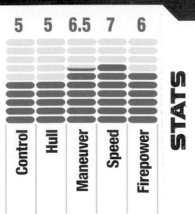

STATS

5	5	6.5	7	6
Control	Hull	Maneuver	Speed	Firepower

INFO

Ubrikkian Industries	**Manufacturer**
Galactic Empire	**Affiliation**
Armored troop transport	**Type**
8.77 meters long	**Size**
2 forward laser cannons; turret mounted double laser cannon	**Weapons**
150 kph	**Top speed**

Who wins? See page 64.

PHANTOM (VS.) TIE FIGHTER

Faced with endless enemies, the Rebels often rely on surprise. Their trusty starship the *Ghost* is, in fact, two ships in one. With a TIE fighter in close pursuit, the *Phantom* suddenly detaches from the *Ghost*'s tail section to engage the enemy.

PHANTOM

The *Phantom*, which docks into the *Ghost*'s tail section, has forward-facing laser cannons operated by its pilot, as well as a small remote-operated turret on its roof. It has a single-seat, fighter-like cockpit, and a small passenger section with fold-down seats.

INFO	
Manufacturer	Corellian Engineering Corporation
Affiliation	Rebel
Type	Custom modified auxiliary shuttle/starfighter
Size	11.63 meters long
Weapons	2 forward laser cannons; 1 dorsal laser turret
Top speed	1,200 kph (in atmosphere)

STATS

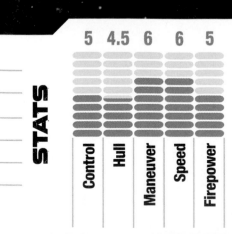

Control	Hull	Maneuver	Speed	Firepower
5	4.5	6	6	5

THE SHOWDOWN

When docked with the *Ghost*, the *Phantom*'s forward cannons are locked in a single position. As the *Phantom* separates from its mother ship, pilot Kanan Jarrus now has full control of its defenses. The small ship darts away, drawing the TIE fighter's attention. A starfighter-on-starfighter dogfight breaks out.

IMPERIAL TIE FIGHTER

The current TIE model is a design that is always undergoing review and improvement by skilled engineers. However, the manufacturer Sienar Fleet Systems faces tight budgets imposed by the Empire, which keeps them from making many improvements.

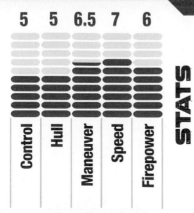

STATS

Control	5
Hull	5
Maneuver	6.5
Speed	7
Firepower	6

INFO

Sienar Fleet Systems	**Manufacturer**
Galactic Empire	**Affiliation**
Twin ion engine space superiority fighter	**Type**
5.33 meters long	**Size**
2 laser cannons	**Weapons**
1,200 kph (in atmosphere)	**Top speed**

Who wins? See page 64.

SPOTLIGHT ON WEAPONRY

THE INQUISITOR'S LIGHTSABER

The Inquisitor carries a uniquely modified lightsaber to give him an unfair advantage in combat. The disc-shaped handle is thirty-nine centimeters in length, and has blade emitters on both ends. Its deadliest secret is that the blade emitters can detach from the central handle, and spin along the outer edge of the disc, turning the lightsaber into a whirling vortex of deadly energy.

KANAN'S LIGHTSABER

Knowing how dangerous it is to be a Jedi in the time of the Empire, Kanan has modified his lightsaber so it can be easily disassembled and stored as innocent-looking gadgets on his belt. When pieced together, it becomes a blue-bladed lightsaber with a handle forty-four centimeters long.

SABINE'S BLASTER PISTOLS

Sabine is well educated in the field of electronics and munitions. She has applied these talents as well as her creative flair into her paired blaster pistols by giving them increased power efficiency (so they last longer between recharges) and more accuracy.

ZEB'S BO-RIFLE

Zeb carries his bo-rifle proudly, as it was once the style of weapon used by the Lasat honor guard. In addition to being a long-range blaster, the bo-rifle unfolds to reveal energized electro-staff tips that, in an expert warrior's hand, becomes a close-combat weapon.

Some Imperials may view a posting on so remote a world as Lothal as punishment. But the frontier offers opportunities for an ambitious young Imperial to make a name for himself. Supply Master Lyste is not about to let some rim-world bumpkins stand in the way of his advancement.

SUPPLY MASTER LYSTE

Lyste has the difficult job of keeping the Imperial forces well-equipped on a remote outpost. In addition to overseeing weapons shipments, Lyste keeps track of the weapons and gear that are built by Lothal workers. A sterling example of an ambitious young Imperial, Lyste is methodical and humorless.

INFO

Homeworld	Garei
Affiliation	Galactic Empire
Species	Human
Height/Weight	1.81 meters/75 kilograms
Weapons	Blaster pistol
Special move	Academy uppercut

STATS

Intelligence	Strength	Agility	Damage	Control	Courage
7	5	5	5	5.5	6

THE SHOWDOWN

Tsoklo's horrible habit of throwing his imagined authority around has turned against him. Hateful neighbors have spread whispers of him hoarding food. These rumors reach Lyste, and a surprise inspection of Tsoklo's house finds a stash of grain the Rodian planned to sell on the black market. Lyste attempts to arrest Tsoklo, but the desperate Rodian pulls a blade.

TSOKLO

To protect himself, Tsoklo helps out the Empire by reporting to Lyste when fellow factory workers aren't as productive as they can be, or when he hears of citizens bending the rules. Tsoklo bullies his neighbors by boasting about having a friend in the Imperial ranks.

STATS

	5.5	5	6	4.5	5	3
	Intelligence	Strength	Agility	Damage	Control	Courage

INFO

Lothal	**Homeworld**
Galactic Empire	**Affiliation**
Rodian	**Species**
1.79 meters/72 kilograms	**Height/Weight**
Utility vibroblade	**Weapons**
Panicked flail	**Special move**

Who wins? See page 64.

For centuries, Lothal quietly existed on the periphery of galactic affairs. Its proud settlers turned the fertile grasslands into productive farms to feed their families and villages. When the Empire arrived, many of the soldiers assumed Lothal was their property to do with as they pleased.

AT-DP PILOT

Guiding the massive Imperial walker over uneven terrain requires the skill of seasoned drivers. Although they undergo rigorous training, walker pilots are often looked upon with disdain by stormtroopers, who envy their elevated perches and protective cockpits of reinforced armor.

INFO

Homeworld	Various
Affiliation	Galactic Empire
Species	Various
Height/Weight	Average 1.83 meters/80 kilograms
Weapons	E-11 blaster rifle
Special move	Targeted strike

STATS

Intelligence	Strength	Agility	Damage	Control	Courage
5	6	5	5	5	8

THE SHOWDOWN

A belligerent AT-DP pilot strolls through the Kothal marketplace, feeling invincible in his helmet and chest armor. Feeling hungry and ready for a fight, he orders Sumar to give him a ripe, juicy jogan fruit. Sumar refuses unless he is paid for the fruit, which only makes the AT-DP pilot angrier. Not wanting Sumar to set an example of defiance, the pilot pulls out his blaster pistol.

MORAD SUMAR

A local farmer, Morad Sumar tends his fields outside of the town of Kothal. The property's enviable location near a major vein of ore has caused the Empire to take interest in Sumar's land. Sumar was born and raised on Lothal, and embodies the fierce, independent spirit of the Lothal farmer.

STATS

Intelligence	6
Strength	5
Agility	3
Damage	3
Control	3
Courage	8

INFO

Homeworld	Lothal
Affiliation	His farm and family
Species	Human
Height/Weight	1.84 meters/75 kilograms
Weapons	Hunting blaster
Special move	Braced and steadily aimed shot

Who wins? See page 64.

LOTH-CAT ⬤VS.⬤ FYRNOCK

The fur will fly as this fanged fight erupts in the dark corner of an unattended docking bay. A wild loth-cat sniffing around for food has attracted the attention of an illegally smuggled fyrnock, a nasty-tempered critter found on a nearby asteroid ring.

LOTH-CAT

The loth-cat is a breed of tooka that has adapted to the tall grasses of Lothal. It is a nimble hunter with sharp teeth and claws. A loth-cat may often scurry from a fight, but when cornered, it will hiss, spit, scratch, and bite a much larger opponent.

INFO

Homeworld	Lothal
Length/Weight	0.94 meters/10 kilograms
Weapons	Sharp teeth, claws
Special move	Attack crouch pounce

STATS

Intelligence	Strength	Agility	Damage	Control	Courage
3	4.5	9	5	6	7

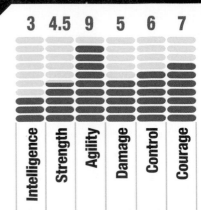

THE SHOWDOWN

Sensing the body temperature of prey nearby, the fyrnock bursts from its unguarded crate and leaps at the loth-cat. The clatter of the crate lid alerts the loth-cat to the danger. In the darkened docking bay, the loth-cat puffs out its fur to look more dangerous and stares down the red eyes peering from the shadows.

FYRNOCK

A small, hardy creature that evolved to survive under harsh conditions on asteroids with thin atmospheres, the fyrnock often enters a deep sleep. When disturbed, it will emerge from its slumber with ravenous energy. Fyrnocks hate sunlight, so they are far more dangerous in the dark.

STATS

Intelligence	2
Strength	5
Agility	8
Damage	6
Control	5
Courage	6

INFO

Homeworld	Various asteroid hives
Length/Weight	2.48 meters/15 kilograms
Weapons	Sharp teeth, claws
Special move	Slashing strike

Who wins? See page 64.

CIKATRO VIZAGO (VS.) WULLFFWARRO

Cikatro Vizago once helped out Wullffwarro's band of Wookiees by selling information that led to their rescue from Imperial clutches. But that doesn't make them friends—especially not when there are credits involved.

CIKATRO VIZAGO

Cikatro Vizago is the most well-connected scoundrel in all of Lothal. His own survival and profit are his top priority. The crew of the *Ghost* runs the occasional errand for Vizago, because his Broken Horn gang pays well and isn't likely to alert Imperial authorities.

INFO

Homeworld	Devaron
Affiliation	Broken Horn gang
Species	Devaronian
Height/Weight	2.02 meters/84 kilograms
Weapons	Heavy blaster pistol; spiked knuckles
Special move	Charging headbutt

STATS

Intelligence	Strength	Agility	Damage	Control	Courage
6	7	4.5	5	7	5

THE SHOWDOWN

Vizago has heard tell of a Trandoshan hunter willing to pay big credits for a Wookiee pelt. Knowing where to find the Wookiee unawares, Vizago shadows a sleepy, well-fed Wullffwarro as he wanders back to his ship from a spaceport eatery. Knowing the Trandoshan will pay extra if the fur is unsinged, Vizago dials his blaster to stun and takes aim.

WULLFFWARRO

A local leader on Kashyyyk and veteran of the Clone Wars, Wullffwarro has deep appreciation for the ways of the Jedi Knights and the ideals of the Old Republic. He and his clan try to avoid the attention of the Empire.

STATS

5	11	4	8	5	6.5
Intelligence	Strength	Agility	Damage	Control	Courage

INFO

Kashyyyk	**Homeworld**
His village	**Affiliation**
Wookiee	**Species**
2.23 meters/115 kilograms	**Height/Weight**
None	**Weapons**
Arm-ripper pull	**Special move**

Who wins? See page 64.

DEV MORGAN (VS.) ZARE LEONIS

In the training arenas of the Lothal Imperial Academy, the strict taskmasters teach young students that friendship is a weakness. The drive to win is what matters the most. The instructors pit the cadets against one another, rewarding those that rise above the rest.

DEV MORGAN

Dev Morgan is a mystery, having arrived at the Academy with a wave of new cadets. Although Dev doesn't talk about his past, he is hardly shy. He is a very competitive cadet whose boastful nature is backed by excellent coordination and reflexes.

INFO	
Homeworld	Lothal
Affiliation	Unknown
Species	Human
Height/Weight	1.65 meters/50 kilograms
Weapons	None
Special move	Dodge-and-roll

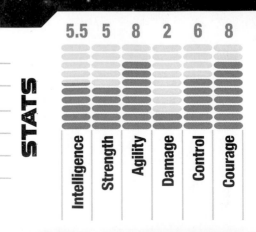

STATS					
5.5	5	8	2	6	8
Intelligence	Strength	Agility	Damage	Control	Courage

THE SHOWDOWN

The swaggering Taskmaster Grint barks a challenge at the awaiting cadets. They must navigate an obstacle course of floating platforms, jumping from each one in numbered order, to reach the highest platform where a training blaster pistol sits. The first to reach the blaster and stun the other opponent into submission wins.

ZARE LEONIS

A star student at the Academy, Zare is smart and athletic. He exhibits true leadership skills. Unlike many of his fellow cadets, he is reserved and not prone to bragging. He is intensely focused on achievement, and follows in the footsteps of his older sister, who also attended the Academy.

STATS

6.5	5.5	7.5	2	6	9
Intelligence	Strength	Agility	Damage	Control	Courage

INFO

Lothal	**Homeworld**
Galactic Empire	**Affiliation**
Human	**Species**
1.65 meters/50 kilograms	**Height/Weight**
None	**Weapons**
Long jump-and-evade	**Special move**

Who wins? See page 64.

AMDA WABO (VS.) MAKETH TUA

An Imperial government official on Lothal, Maketh Tua meets with Amda Wabo, a representative from a nearby world. Wabo hopes to negotiate a sale of experimental weapons to the Empire. A misunderstanding has caused Wabo to think Tua double-crossed him.

AMDA WABO

The Aqualish weapons manufacturer is very cautious, as his line of business often places him in dangerous company. He would be more comfortable with bodyguard droids, but he has agreed to a one-on-one meeting to prevent Tua from bringing stormtroopers.

INFO

Homeworld	Ando
Affiliation	Independent
Species	Aqualish
Height/Weight	1.67 meters/80 kilograms
Weapons	Heavy blaster pistol
Special move	Belligerent shove

STATS

Intelligence	Strength	Agility	Damage	Control	Courage
7	5.5	5.5	6	6	5

THE SHOWDOWN

In addition to his restriction on the presence of armed guards, Amda Wabo insisted on no droids. But Wabo doesn't speak the common language, and Minister Tua cannot speak Aqualish. Without a protocol droid to translate, their meeting grows hostile. Tua's efforts to calm Wabo fail, and the Aqualish draws his heavy blaster pistol.

MAKETH TUA

Having studied abroad on worlds more cosmopolitan than her native Lothal, Maketh Tua considers herself above the people of a "barely civilized Outer Rim world." She enjoys the refined conversation of fellow intellectuals, and resents having to deal with unsavory types in her Imperial duties.

STATS

8	4.5	5.5	5	6	6.5
Intelligence	Strength	Agility	Damage	Control	Courage

INFO

Lothal	**Homeworld**
Galactic Empire	**Affiliation**
Human	**Species**
1.87 meters/55 kilograms	**Height/Weight**
Holdout blaster pistol	**Weapons**
Crushing heel stomp	**Special move**

Who wins? See page 64.

A well-traveled starpilot who has logged as many parsecs as Hera Syndulla can attest to the natural dangers of the galaxy. Asteroids, cosmic storms, planetary weather, and even native animal life can prove just as dangerous as Imperial patrols.

PHANTOM

The compact *Phantom* starfighter is agile and can be easily maneuvered through canyons and the tight spaces of uncharted worlds. In this way, the *Phantom* serves as a scout ship in addition to a secret starfighter.

INFO

Manufacturer	Corellian Engineering Corporation
Affiliation	Rebel
Type	Custom modified auxiliary shuttle/starfighter
Size	11.63 meters long
Weapons	2 forward laser cannons; 1 dorsal laser turret
Top speed	1,200 kph (in atmosphere)

STATS

Control	Hull	Maneuver	Speed	Firepower
5	4.5	6	6	5

THE SHOWDOWN

An intensely curious tibidee casts a shadow over the *Phantom*. The electronic signature of the *Phantom*'s sensor systems sound like an invitation to the massive creature to play, so Hera switches off as much as she can, having to rely on her eyes and instincts to navigate the *Phantom*'s cannons.

TIBIDEE

The tibidee is an enormous gasbag flier, remotely related to such creatures as the neebrays and mynocks. These leathery winged giants live in the peaks of several mountainous worlds in the Outer Rim Territories. They are occasionally attracted to the electronic signals broadcast by starships.

STATS

4	3	7	4.5	1
Control	Hull	Maneuver	Speed	Firepower

INFO

Various	**Homeworld**
16.17 meters/750 kilograms	**Length/Weight**
Enormous body mass	**Weapons**
700 kph (in right atmosphere)	**Top speed**

Who wins?
See page 64.

R2-D2 has witnessed many pivotal moments in galactic history, but he rarely processes their significance because he is primarily focused on loyally carrying out the instructions of his master. He lets nothing get in his way, not even a stubbornly malfunctioning RX pilot droid.

R2-D2

Devoted to duty and possessing a spirit of adventure, R2-D2 is a resourceful and reliable astromech droid. He's loaded with all sorts of gizmos, graspers, and tools that let him repair and manipulate a wide variety of technology—such as computers, door locks, and coded transmissions.

INFO

Homeworld	Naboo
Affiliation	Royal House of Alderaan
Manufacturer	Industrial Automaton
Height/Weight	1.1 meters/32 kilograms
Weapons	Electroshock prod, circular saw, arc welder
Special move	Shock

STATS

Intelligence	Strength	Agility	Damage	Control	Courage
5.5	4	4	5	6	8

THE SHOWDOWN

R2-D2 is under orders to deliver Imperial data intercepted on Lothal to the Alderaanian embassy on Adarlon. The fastest way there is to take a commuter shuttle, but the stubborn RX droid has a programming glitch that is keeping the ship grounded. When R2-D2 rolls up to the cockpit, hoping to take control of the ship, the malfunctioning RX droid puts up a fight.

RX-SERIES PILOT DROID

A navigator and pilot droid, the RX unit is installed in the cockpits of transport vessels. These chipper, talkative droids are meant to interact with passengers on commuter starships, and offer helpful travel information and safety tips.

STATS

6	5	2	5	4	7
Intelligence	Strength	Agility	Damage	Control	Courage

INFO

Nubia	**Homeworld**
Garel Interstellar Excursions	**Affiliation**
Industrial Automaton	**Manufacturer**
1.26 meters/55 kilograms	**Height/Weight**
None	**Weapons**
Swiveling clawed arm swipe	**Special move**

Who wins? See page 64.

While R2-D2 tangles with a malfunctioning pilot droid in his mission to leave Lothal, his counterpart, C-3PO, realizes the shuttle must get past a procedure-minded protocol droid in charge of managing departures at the Lothal spaceport.

C-3PO

A protocol droid fluent in over six million forms of communication, C-3PO is unaware of his origins on Tatooine or whom he formerly served. His memory was wiped upon becoming Captain Antilles's droid, where he unknowingly helps Bail Organa's secret work against the Empire.

INFO

Homeworld	Tatooine
Affiliation	Royal House of Alderaan
Manufacturer	Anakin Skywalker—Cybot Galactica
Height/Weight	1.77 meters/75 kilograms
Weapons	None
Special move	Capable of begging for mercy in over 6 million forms of communication

STATS

Intelligence	Strength	Agility	Damage	Control	Courage
7.5	4	2.5	1	3	4

THE SHOWDOWN

Worried he will fail R2-D2 and his master Captain Antilles, C-3PO shuffles into the spaceport control station. At first, C-3PO tries to talk his way past the Lothal protocol droid, claiming he carries a command override from Governor Pryce herself. The controller droid does not believe the lie. C-3PO must act quickly before the other droid calls the authorities.

LOTHAL PROTOCOL DROID

This protocol model is a common droid in the systems that surround Lothal. They are built and programmed locally for service in government and private business offices. They have many of the same features and functions found on more expensive protocol droids found in the areas of the galaxy.

STATS	
Intelligence	7
Strength	4
Agility	2
Damage	1
Control	3
Courage	3.5

INFO	
Homeworld	Lothal
Affiliation	Lothal Port Authority
Manufacturer	Lothal Logistics Limited
Height/Weight	1.85 meters/75 kilograms
Weapons	None
Special move	Emergency comlink call to Lothal authorities

Who wins? See page 64.

THE COMING STORM . . .

Following the chaos of the Clone Wars, there has been peace in the galaxy for over a decade. The Empire maintained control of the galaxy and grew in power. As the spirit of rebellion spreads, the galaxy inches toward the brink of civil war. Heroes determined to bring back the ideals of justice and freedom are preparing to strike back.

Some of these conflicts are personal rather than political. Some heroes carry grudges against the Empire based on the actions of specific soldiers and officers. Other heroes are driven by the will of the Force.

When the Emperor came to power, he and Darth Vader wiped out the Jedi Knights, leaving the Force in darkness. But the Force strives for balance, and the heroes of the light will rise again to challenge the dark side. There will come new heroes to champion peace and justice as the Jedi once did, and their fire will return to the galaxy.

ZEB ORRELIOS (VS.) AGENT KALLUS

Zeb Orrelios flies into a rage when he sees Agent Kallus striding onto the battlefield. The armored agent brandishes a weapon that clearly started off as a Lasat bo-rifle before being modified for Imperial use.

GARAZEB "ZEB" ORRELIOS

Zeb is one of the last Lasat in the galaxy to carry the weapon of the honor guard, the versatile bo-rifle. When the Empire conquered his home planet, Lasan, they did so swiftly and violently, wiping out many of the planet's citizens. The Lasan honor guard fought hard, but proved to be no match for the Imperial forces.

INFO

Homeworld	Lasan
Affiliation	Rebel
Species	Lasat
Height/Weight	2.1 meters/115 kilograms
Weapons	Lasat bo-rifle
Special move	Whirlwind throw

STATS

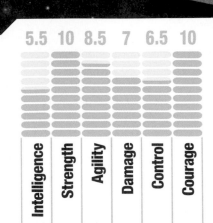

Intelligence	Strength	Agility	Damage	Control	Courage
5.5	10	8.5	7	6.5	10

THE SHOWDOWN

Kallus is confident. He has spent years training his body into fighting shape, and is quick to battle a Lasat with a weapon he admires very much. Kallus would consider it a point of pride to defeat Zeb, and Zeb feels it is his duty to take down this Imperial. Kallus sneers at Zeb, calling out the Lasat. Zeb roars back a challenge, igniting the ends of his bo-rifle and charging into battle.

AGENT KALLUS

As a reaction to escalating reports of rebel activity on Lothal, the Empire dispatched an agent from the Imperial Security Bureau. Kallus is a skilled pilot and an extremely capable combatant, even able to go toe-to-toe with a powerful brawler like Zeb.

STATS

8	9	7	6.5	7	10
Intelligence	Strength	Agility	Damage	Control	Courage

INFO

Coruscant	**Homeworld**
Galactic Empire	**Affiliation**
Human	**Species**
1.95 meters/90 kilograms	**Height/Weight**
Modified Lasat bo-rifle	**Weapons**
Twirling staff strike	**Special move**

Who wins? See page 64.

KANAN & EZRA (VS.) THE INQUISITOR

While investigating rebel activity on Lothal, the Imperial Security Bureau reported evidence of someone using a lightsaber. Following up on these intriguing incidents, the Inquisitor hunts a truly rare prize: a master and an apprentice, studying the ways of the Jedi.

KANAN & EZRA

Ezra and Kanan have quickly forged a bond. Recognizing the threat of the Inquisitor, Kanan has begun instructing Ezra in the ways of the Force, so the boy can better defend himself from the dangers of the dark side. Ezra is eager to learn, but finds the lessons of the Jedi (and working with Kanan) challenging.

INFO

	KANAN	EZRA
Homeworld	Unknown	Lothal
Affiliation	Rebel	Rebel
Species	Human	Human
Height/Weight	1.91 m/80 kg	1.65 m/50 kg
Weapons	Lightsaber	Lightsaber
Special move	Behind-the-back parry and strike	Dodge-and-roll

STATS

	Intelligence	Strength	Agility	Damage	Control	Courage
	5.5	5	8	5	6	10
	6.5	8	7	7.5	6.5	8

THE SHOWDOWN

The Inquisitor sees the raw, reckless potential of Ezra, who has only just begun practicing with his newly constructed lightsaber. Although Ezra has learned much from Kanan, the two are inexperienced at working together. The Inquisitor taunts Ezra, telling him the path to true power can be found on the dark side.

THE INQUISITOR

The Inquisitor relishes the discovery that Kanan is a Jedi who has found and taken on a young Force-sensitive as an apprentice. Two such targets are a valuable prize for the dark enforcer. The Inquisitor has already assessed Kanan's fighting style. The boy is an unknown, but the Inquisitor is a fast learner.

STATS					
9.5	8.5	8.5	8	9	10
Intelligence	Strength	Agility	Damage	Control	Courage

INFO	
Unknown, presumably Utapau	**Homeworld**
Galactic Empire	**Affiliation**
Pau'an	**Species**
1.98 meters/80 kilograms	**Height/Weight**
Modified double-bladed lightsaber	**Weapons**
Spinning lightsaber throw	**Special move**

Who wins? See page 64.

GHOST VS. THE INQUISITOR'S TIE ADVANCED

After hastily escaping the Inquisitor's reach, the crew of the *Ghost* scrambles aboard their trusty freighter and blasts off into the skies over Lothal. Undeterred, the Inquisitor gives chase aboard his custom TIE fighter.

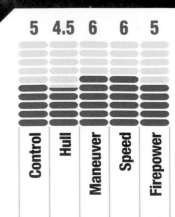

GHOST

The more active the rebels are in their operations around Lothal, the quicker they burn through false aliases for the *Ghost*. Now Imperial patrols carefully inspect any VCX-100 freighter that deviates from a flight path. The crew must be prepared for combat at a moment's notice.

INFO

Manufacturer	Corellian Engineering Corporation
Affiliation	Rebel
Type	Modified VCX-100 light freighter
Size	43.9 meters long
Weapons	1 dorsal laser turret; 2 forward laser cannons; 2 rear laser cannons
Top speed	1,025 kph (in atmosphere)

STATS

Control	Hull	Maneuver	Speed	Firepower
5	4.5	6	6	5

THE SHOWDOWN

Hera pushes the *Ghost*'s engines at full power, but the tenacious TIE prototype stays on the *Ghost*'s tail. The rebel fighter craft's modified engines push the ship faster, stretching the distance between them and the TIE fighter. Kanan mans the top turret, while Ezra jumps into the rear-facing *Phantom*.

THE INQUISITOR'S TIE ADVANCED

The Inquisitor has access to the latest technology to carry out his duty for the Empire. His TIE Advanced prototype features faster engines, S-foils with more efficient solar gather panels, more powerful laser cannons, and a projectile launcher that can fire tracking devices onto fleeing vessels.

STATS

6	4.5	7	7.5	5.5
Control	Hull	Maneuver	Speed	Firepower

INFO

Sienar Fleet Systems	**Manufacturer**
Galactic Empire	**Affiliation**
Experimental twin ion engine space superiority fighter	**Type**
3.57 meters long	**Size**
2 laser cannons	**Weapons**
1,600 kph (in atmosphere)	**Top speed**

Who wins? See page 64.

THE EXPERTS' PICKS

p. 6–7

Ezra Bridger vs. Imperial stormtrooper

The Winner: Ezra Bridger
The stormtrooper is surprised by Ezra's defiance—most locals surrender at any sign of trouble. Ezra's stinging jolts send energy streaking across the trooper's armor, zapping him between the plates and knocking him out.

p. 8–9

Sabine Wren vs. Commandant Aresko

The Winner: Sabine Wren
Even though Aresko just finished lecturing a class full of cadets on the importance of marksmanship, he misses every shot he takes, allowing her to take him down.

p. 10–11

Zeb Orrelios vs. Taskmaster Grint

The Winner: Zeb
Grint is not in the best shape and gets winded going toe-to-toe with a Lasat honor guard. Zeb body slams Grint until the Imperial begs for mercy.

p. 12–13

Kanan Jarrus vs. The Inquisitor

The Winner: The Inquisitor
Kanan was simply not ready for this confrontation. The Inquisitor accurately gauges Kanan's skills and counters his every move. The dark warrior emerges from the duel victorious.

p. 14–15

Hera Syndulla vs. TIE fighter pilot

The Winner: Hera Syndulla
The TIE pilot is convinced he will soundly defeat this insurgent in the air, but he is outclassed in close combat. Hera lands a kick that sends the pilot's black flight helmet spinning.

p. 16–17

Chopper vs. Lothal astromech droid

The Winner: Chopper
Chopper shows no mercy. Spinning his head as he charges, Chopper delivers a flurry of smacks from his upper arms, which crack the other astromech's dome, causing it to retreat.

p. 18–19

IG-RM thug droid vs. Old Jho

The Winner: IG-RM thug droid
Old Jho's spirit is willing, but age has taken a toll on his muscles and reflexes. The thug droid overpowers the aged Ithorian. If only the rebels were there to help!

p. 22–23

Ghost vs. TIE fighter

The Winner: Ghost
The Imperial advantage in starfighter combat is numerical superiority. With only one TIE fighter to contend with, the *Ghost* outmaneuvers its lone opponent and blasts it to cinders.

p. 24–25

Imperial speeder bike vs. AT-DP

The Winner: Imperial speeder bike
Though the bike's guns can't dent the hull of the armored walker, a daring pilot like Sabine points the speeder straight at the AT-DP leg assembly, and jumps for safety. When the bike hits the walker's legs, the resulting explosion causes the walker to collapse.

p. 26–27

jumpspeeder vs. RGC landspeeder

The Winner: jumpspeeder
The rebels pride themselves on taking down larger targets. Sabine's skillfully blasts the RGC speeder with her twin blasters while steering with her knees, crippling the bigger vehicle.

p. 28–29

Wookiee gunship vs. Imperial freighter

The Winner: Wookiee gunship
Though smaller than the freighter, the Wookiee vessel outguns the Imperial ship, which can only aim a single turret on its enemy at a time. The Wookiee cannons tear through the freighter as they escape.

p. 30–31

C-ROC carrier ship vs. Imperial Star Destroyer

The Winner: Imperial Star Destroyer
Although the C-ROC flies wildly to avoid being hit by the Star Destroyer's cannons that fill its flight path with bursts of destructive energy, it is not fast enough to dodge all the weapon fire. A glancing blow sends it spinning out of control.

p. 32–33

V-35 landspeeder vs. Imperial troop transport

The Winner: Imperial troop transport
The transport's thick armor holds as the speeder crumples in the collision. Even when the V-35's power plant explodes, the transport emerges through the smoke and fire unscathed.

p. 34–35

Phantom vs. TIE fighter

The Winner: Phantom
The *Phantom*'s speed and Kanan's reflexes allow it to stay several moves ahead of the TIE fighter's cannons, letting it slip behind the enemy ship and blow it away.

p. 38–39

Supply Master Lyste vs. Tsoklo

The Winner: Supply Master Lyste
A spineless collaborator, Tsoklo cowardly throws himself on the Empire's mercy, only to discover it has none.

p. 40–41

AT-DP pilot vs. Morad Sumar

The Winner: Morad Sumar
Morad refuses to surrender, so the pilot tries to club him with his gun. Twisting out of the pilot's reach, Morad pushes the jogan fruit into the helmeted face of the Imperial. The squishy pulp of the fruit blocks the pilot's lenses, letting Sumar knock him over.

p. 42–43

loth-cat vs. fyrnock

The Winner: loth-cat
The confrontation is violent, but the loth-cat manages to move the fight with the shadow predator into the sunlight. There, the fyrnock cringes at the brightness, and the loth-cat attacks.

p. 44–45

Cikatro Vizago vs. Wullffwarro

The Winner: Wullffwarro
The stun effect engulfs the Wookiee, but Wullffwarro's furious surprise only wakes him up. He charges at the Devaronian, thrashing him so soundly Cikatro should probably rename his gang "The Broken Bones."

p. 46–47

Dev Morgan vs. Zare Leonis

The Winner: Dev Morgan
Though Zare is in peak physical shape, Dev shows an incredible knack at predicting where the platforms will be. With good sportsmanship, Zare concedes defeat, but decides he'll have to keep an eye on this newbie Dev Morgan.

p. 48–49

Amda Wabo vs. Maketh Tua

The Winner: Amda Wabo
Though both combatants are more bureaucrats than warriors, Wabo has had more firsthand experience with armed conflict than the cultured Maketh Tua.

p. 50–51

Phantom vs. tibidee

The Winner: Phantom
Hera refuses to open fire on the innocent creature, so it's a matter of outrunning the beast. It's a close call, but she pilots the ship out of the canyon with only a few scratches and drool stains on the hull.

p. 52–53

R2-D2 vs. RX-series pilot droid

The Winner: R2-D2
R2-D2 will not take no for an answer, and weathers a flurry of RX's slaps before he shuts down the pilot with a well-aimed shock prod.

p. 54–55

C-3PO vs. Lothal protocol droid

The Winner: C-3PO
C-3PO shows an uncharacteristic burst of initiative when facing down an unintimidating opponent, and shoves the droid away from the launch controls, sending it crashing down a set of stairs.

p. 58–59

Zeb Orrelios vs. Agent Kallus

The Winner: Agent Kallus
Kallus knows how to push Zeb's buttons. The enraged Lasat is too angry to concentrate, and Kallus takes advantage of Zeb's rushed attacks to get the upper hand.

p. 60–61

Kanan & Ezra vs. The Inquisitor

The Winner: The Inquisitor
Kanan and Ezra need to work better as a team if they are to beat the Inquisitor. The dark warrior can sense his advantage, and the two heroes barely escape.

p. 62–63

Ghost vs. The Inquisitor's TIE Advanced

The Winner: Ghost
It is a shot fired by Ezra from the *Phantom*'s rear guns that knocks the TIE out of pursuit. The Inquisitor is forced to slow down and slip out of firing range, which lets the *Ghost* leap into hyperspace.